On
Confused
Love

and
Other
Damages

MAGED ZAHER

On Confused Love

and Other Damages

A Novella

CHATWIN
BOOKS

ISBN: 9781633981539

Chatwin Books
www.chatwinbooks.com

This is a work of fiction; all events and characters described here do not, and probably should not, match reality.

To you, mom, as always.

A book about incompletions:
Incomplete jobs,
Incomplete loves,
Incomplete revolutions,
And, naturally, incomplete books.

"Tell, don't show."
—Maged Zaher in conversation with Ramy Keddis

2013

It all started at a regular one-on-one meeting. His boss told him, "It is time for us to go separate ways. It is not your performance, but there used to be this look in your eyes, and it is not there anymore."

The heavily romantic language he was fired with was beautiful.

Sitting across from his boss, Ramy was not sure what to feel. He was always not sure what to feel, but getting fired for the first time in his life opened up a new territory for him to be not sure what to feel about. We can say it broadened his uncertainty horizon. He was grateful for that.

The boss—strangely—started tearing up. As if he was the one being fired. Ramy calmed him. Told him it is okay to fire me. This is life. Well, to be exact, Ramy said "c'est la vie."

Five months later, getting the news that the software department is not doing well after he left, Ramy texted his boss "did you fuck it up you idiot?"—only to feel bad and send a retraction one minute later "sorry, I meant racist idiot."

The boss and Ramy discussed the layoff (a more polite way to say firing)—specifically what tasks Ramy needed to finish before leaving. The boss informed Ramy that he was to meet Jean, the vice president of Human Resources, to learn about the details of the firing and severance package he would get for surviving for seven years in Duvall Media.

"I'm flying to Austin tomorrow, and will meet with Jean when I am back on Monday."

This was the way Ramy was able to restore some of his dignity. Mentioning that he is flying to Austin to perform in a poetry reading and to meet Lia. The woman he had daydreamed about since he met her in Seattle at the Modern Language Association (MLA) conference.

Ramy left B's office and stepped out of the building to take a walk through Seattle's Chinatown.

He went to Uwajimaya, bought an expensive unfiltered sake bottle, and sat on a street bench sipping its white milk while not feeling and not thinking, something his meditation teacher would have been very proud of him for.

Ramy, half an hour earlier, could have been described as:

1. An immigrant.
2. A poet.
3. A Vice President of an average Seattle software company.

An immigrant is someone who is mired in departures. A more neutral way to express an immigrant's departures is to say "false starts."

An immigrant's birth in a different country is the first of these false starts.

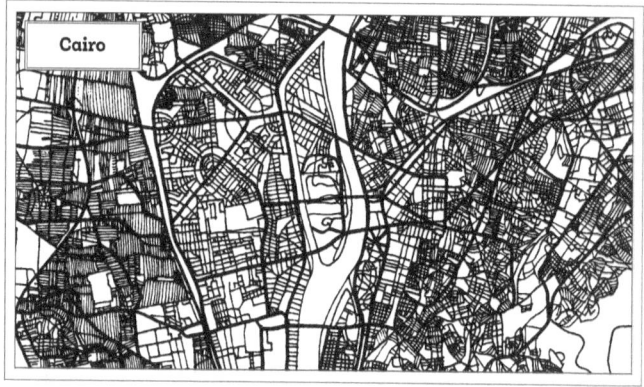

The beginning of longing

"A poet is someone who peels their skin, to let people bathe in their blood."

Ramy memorized Sergei Yesenin's over-the-top definition of what a poet is. He first read this definition translated into Arabic at the age of sixteen and it suited his mood.

He later memorized many poems, and many more sophisticated definitions of poetry. Yet this masochistic image of the need to peel one's skin always felt true. What people do with the poet's blood (most likely not sipping it) is immaterial and of no consequence to the said act of peeling. The poet will peel their own skin just because they want to seduce the world.

Later, Ramy would think of poets as mere technicians of language. Just people who do the maintenance and repairs and upgrades needed to keep language alive, since engineers and politicians and business people seem to continuously use language in a way that causes significant wear and tear.

Most of the wounds were not
surprising. They came from
driving Toyotas and Hondas
to work early every day and
from taking work calls
in the middle of dinner.
Ah, this intense flexibility,
that comes with foreignness:
"for the gentiles, a gentile, for
the Jews, a Jew" damaged
and expanded Ramy. He can
navigate a conversation with
many people, he would
resurrect a part of
himself that is appropriate
for the conversation.
Ramy, expanded and flexible
to the point of core-lessness.

After the no-longer-vice-president-of-software-architecture finished the sake bottle, he changed his mind, and went to Jean's office. Jean: a beautiful woman and skilled pimp. The two great qualities needed to run the human resource department in an average Seattle software company.

Pimping to the cruel executives was Jean's duty and she excelled at it. Jean and her staff excelled at pretending to be each employee's friend, until the laying-off moment comes.

Ramy sat across from Jean like the obedient employee he was, and being a little drunk helped him put a ridiculous smile on his face. The same smile he kept—out of helplessness—when he was yelled at or insulted as a young boy in his first country. This smile was even more ridiculous than ever, he had to pretend again—"I am okay. I am a big boy. You think you are humiliating me, but I am above that." While knowing well this time—as he always knew—that he isn't really okay, that this humiliation is touching his core, and that he is just smiling because he can't do much else.

Ramy's excitement about the Austin trip was now mixed with shame.

A few months later, all his emotions would recede and get replaced with anger.

It was 2011, and the Arab Spring that had just happened, was the backdrop of the MLA conference held in Seattle.

As it turns out, one person's revolution is another's career opportunity. Academicians were struggling with analyses and explanations of the Arab Spring. Grants were flying around for anyone who could speak a bit of broken Arabic. American academia accepted the task the American public needed it to answer—"How come we didn't predict these revolutions?"

Unpacking the assumptions behind this question is a topic for an essay, but this is a confused novella or a poem about poets and love and getting unnecessarily fired in the middle of a Thursday.

Ramy and Amina (Ramy's dear Palestinian friend, who was finishing her doctorate in Seattle about storytelling in indigenous communities) were attending an MLA session by a professor who scrambled a paper about the chants of the Arab streets and how they recalled the ancient Arab poets practice of "standing by the ruins." Ramy laughed out loud—Amina, a considerate and kind person, nodded to Ramy approvingly.

The same evening, Ramy and Amina went to the Italian bistro in the Pike Place market, Seattle's famous farmer's market where they throw fish to amuse tourists. Amina ran into Daniel, an Arab-American scholar. Daniel had a zen monk calmness about him, probably from years of smoking weed, and the deep realization that nothing is worth one's anguish. Even an outrageous claim like comparing the Arab chants while revolting in cities, with the romantic gesture of poets standing by the ruins of their beloved departed desert tribes.

Ramy and Amina and Daniel argued about the Arab Spring and the American (and Canadian) academic response to it. Amina pointed out that as orientalism was a reflection of the West projecting its suppressed desires on the exotic East, the Arab Spring papers were a reflection of the political landscape of American politics. Ramy disagreed, "Amina, these are grant seekers, not honorable perverse voyeurs with desires and projections."

He took a sip of some hard liquor and finished his sentence, "This is America, we are allowed to desire only money. It is why we are here, we poor third worlders."

Two Ph.D. students, on the brink of graduation, i.e. job seekers, which is the lowest rank in the MLA circus hierarchy, joined the table—Rana and Lia. They were friends of Daniel, and they were finishing their doctorates from UC Berkeley.

Both Rana and Lia are tall, both were in tight jeans and leather boots. Rana, dark skinned with dark eyes and fast words. Lia, fair skinned, blue eyes, and she uttered her words after thinking through them.

Ramy, despite his ambivalence about academia, was always fascinated by scholars, the ability of one person to give years of their lives to chase one topic to its end. So when Lia sat next to him, he asked her about her research area. She was studying Soviet literature, using de Saussure as her theoretical foundation. Given the events of the day, Ramy was slightly suspicious of yet another American studying the East. He was courteous enough to keep his suspicion hanging while letting himself accept his attraction to Lia's blue eyes, and the way she stuttered her words.

Ramy and Lia found themselves discussing some of the obscure poets of the Soviet Union, she knew these poets because of her scholarly work and she fell in love with them. He knew these poets because he read them as a teenager in the eighties in cheap Arabic translations subsidized by the Soviets and he fell in love with them.

They marveled at Chinghiz Aitmatov, Rasul Gamzatov, and socialist realism.

The group left for their hotels. Ramy and Lia took a couple of steps back and walked next to each other, feeling nostalgic to parts of their past, to Aitmatov and Gamzatov, they were both grateful to each other and to their unexpected conversation in Seattle's downtown midnight streets.

On Saturday, at the bookfair of the MLA, Ramy, carrying a large pile of books, ran into Lia. She was in her cowboy boots again. They said hi, and talked about remaining in touch. As she was leaving, he felt a wave of sadness overtaking his body.

A few months after the Seattle meeting, Ramy saw Lia again in Los Angeles. He read exhausted short poems in a poetry reading run by his friend Andrew McCann. Ramy called these poems Tanakas. He was scared of calling them exhausted poems.

Observing Lia's nonlinear thoughts accumulating at the corner of a bar they went to after the reading, and her stuttering when looking for the exact right word, Ramy felt a return to the sadness he felt seeing her leave the book fair in Seattle a few months earlier.

Lia told him that she is from Texas and her name in the old testament meant "the wandering one," which she said was true as she was obsessed with traveling. Ramy viewed traveling as a privilege for the few, and he breathed better noticing that Lia never bragged about that.

They walked together in the LA winter evening. Andrew and a few others were steps ahead of them. When they passed by a synagogue, Lia commented, "My mom, a baptist, is the best Jew I know"—she was giddy. And they talked about books again, and she told him, "My favorite book ever, is Malek Haddad's *Je t'offrirai une gazelle*," and they decided to translate it together to English. Lia at the end of the night cryptically said, "You live there, and I live nowhere."

Later he would email her, "I think I love you," which she responded to with, "I think I love you too."

Yet later still, way later, Ramy would feel that Lia is everywhere in the world except wherever he is.

Lia didn't go to see Ramy in Austin. And when he texted her, she said that she was busy with job applications.

He couldn't tell her that he was just fired. He didn't want pity, he wanted the "I think it is love" thing that grew between them over multiple meetings in cities they happened to be in coincidentally:

— In NY when she asked a man about the subway, and Ramy stood there feeling helpless as that man was answering Lia with confidence and lust.

— In Berkeley, where they first slept together.

— In Seattle again, where they went to Benaroya Hall to listen to a torturous form of classical music she was into.

— And in Austin, where . . . "Where Lia didn't show up."

Yes, all philosophizing is but language flaws. But with both his job and Lia's disappearance, Ramy had only language to play with its flaws. Turn this language into bodily reactions to combat despair.

With nothing but time to tinker with, Ramy decided to do one of these searching for oneself expeditions he read about in books.

To keep things within an appropriate cliché, he would go search for himself in Cairo, his hometown. He imagined walking his old city streets and visiting churches and sitting in the same coffeeshops he used to frequent as a student in Cairo University, or as a young engineer with the Arab Consulting Engineers, the firm he worked for before immigrating to Amerika.

One of these city walks would eventually and very randomly connect him to a childhood friend, hopefully a woman, she would be going through a different crisis, and they would both fall in love with each other, and solve whatever crisis they were both going through.

The problem is that the Egyptian school system is segregated, and most of his childhood friends were men. This presented a minor caveat that didn't affect the overall plan. The most important thing was that Cairo is definitely cheaper and he would last longer there moneywise.

Ramy approached each sexual encounter as a last meal. Worse, as a last meal that might be taken away if he did anything wrong. So he ended up being a generous and satisfactory lover.

Ramy uttered Lia's name to himself all the time. The letter "ل" or "lam" in Arabic is a luminous letter. Said Ibn Arabi. He also said something like "The lam is a divine secret. It is one of the letters that makes Allah's name. Its nature is warmth and cold and dryness. Its biggest constituent is fire. Its least constituent is dust." The "lam" is a lovely and estranged letter.

Ramy first met Lamya at a party at his friend Dalia's. There was some lunar event that Ramy didn't care much about. He was there for the alcohol and the possibilities.

The moon didn't do what it was supposed to do, but at the end of the night Lamya aggressively asked for his phone number, and they went for a boat ride on the Nile and they talked and talked and he kissed her on a dark Cairo street and she yelled "I wish you were living here!"

<- - - - - - - - - - - - Insert a page about Lamya here

Lamya, as it turned out, was a celebrity. She was a famous Lebanese journalist who had been working in Egypt for a few years by then. She was known for her professional, well-researched yet passionate articles, and was a frequent guest on different TV channels.

Ramy, when a young teenager
in Cairo read Nizar Qabbani,
his poems about Beirut
and Beirutian women. He
also saw lovers walk on
the Nile holding hands. So
with Lamya, being on a
boat on the Nile was the
collapse of the disparate dreams of love
into one. A Beirutian woman
on the Nile. Who said clichés
don't bring happiness!

Two months before the boat ride with Lamya, Lia was wandering Budapest, and being a Marxist, she was naturally in some protest against one of these injustices that fill the earth.

Ramy sent her, "I think I am still in love with you" again, to which she, with her Marxist tendency of equity, replied, "I think I am still in love with you too."

Lamya and Ramy agreed to spend the day together. He visited her apartment carrying the most expensive flowers he ever bought. She opened the door in her nightie, gave him a quick kiss, and continued her phone call with her editor, they were negotiating and gossipping. She waved Ramy to the kitchen and pointed—tea or coffee? He chose the tea, and proceeded with kissing her neck from behind, so as not to interrupt the simultaneous phone call and tea making.

In her balcony that oversees the Nile, they sipped tea and talked about the Egyptian revolution and its aftermath.

Ramy might have been a middle class executive in the US, but in Egypt he was always a poor kid. It wasn't a matter of money, it was a matter of emotions and power structure. Being in an apartment that overlooks the Nile with a woman who is so connected to the powerful elite of the country wasn't something he would have ever dreamt of when he lived in Cairo twenty years earlier. He was now soaking his class mobility with a bit of his old sense of inferiority.

Lamya took Ramy to her
apartment in Zamalek, the
historically bourgeois rich
neighborhood of the
Egyptian bourgeois.
Lia.
Lamya took Ramy to
her apartment in Zamalek,
the famously rich
neighborhood. It has
profound American restaurants
like Arby's and Pizza Hut.
And a knockoff Victoria's
Secret that is called
subtly 69.
They didn't stop instead the
living room, they landed
on her couch in her kiss,
on the gorgeous Balcony.
Ramy likes to fuck sleep.
Lamya was almost
Lia
With rich women,
Ramy is an inverted
gigolo bourgeois. He
steps up his middle-class
spending game and pays
more than he is comfortable

for dinner in expensive
restaurants, just to get
to sleep on a rich
woman's bed.

"There is a World beyond deprivation,"
he explained to Fouad.
Ramy wasn't sure if his connection
with Lamya would go anywhere
but her shape and the way she
kissed him, always never allowing
his mouth to fully rest on
hers, was just perfect.
"But I don't want to witness
anything."
What to do with yourself
once you know there is
a class struggle, and that
you are avoiding it. Which
means you are on the
opposite side of History,
as you read in Marxist propaganda
books when you were sixteen.

Lamya and Ramy went to pick up Jamila, Lamya's daughter from her second marriage, from school, to take her phone shopping.

Jamila didn't like any of the phones, so they gave up and went for dinner instead. Jamila was not happy that she had to go visit her Morrocan dad in Paris. Lamya was very confusing to Jamila, she would advise against the visit yet argue for it. Ramy—armed with good skills from years of undergoing useless talk therapy in Seattle—asked Lamya to give Jamila a chance to talk. He asked Jamila a few open-ended questions so she could process her feelings and needs at ease, and kept blocking Lamya's interruptions of her daughter.

Back on Lamya's balcony, she told him how much she liked how he acted with Jamila. She also said "if you asked me, there, in the restaurant, to marry you, I would have accepted." And started to unzip him. They engaged in physically complex yet delicious sex.

At 3:22 a.m. he received a text message from Lamya that canceled their appointment the next day.

At noon he received another text message from her saying that she had a message from God that they shouldn't be together.

The Lebanese non-practicing Muslim (who was also an active Marxist in the Lebanese communist party in her youth) was in direct contact with the almighty, and he, Ramy, the Copt, wasn't. He was now hit both romantically and spiritually by one text message.

"Does love overlap?"

"Do you ever love more than one person, or are all emotions directed to an archetype?"

He thought to himself that all the women he fell in love with lately seem to have names that start with "L": Lia, the wandering Jew; Lamya, the non-practicing Muslim. Both Marxists. And he—a Copt—with a name that is six steps behind in the alphabet, became acutely aware of his inadequacy.

He went to Lamya's house to talk. She wasn't interested anymore. The message from God actually came in the shape of a call from a Parisian ex-boyfriend. Well, historical materialism was still alive, thank God.

Instead of backing up quickly he indulged his humiliation, and kneeled to kiss her feet. She told him, "Don't torture yourself."

He didn't like the advice, so he stood up and left for a nearby pub to drink and torture himself without distractions.

Packing his bag to get back to Seattle, Ramy spent time listening to Arabic music meowing.

Words are corpses. He dug deep and found he was scared to not be able to fathom existence.

Poetry, work, books, and love were mere obsessions to pass time.

2018

There are things to
abhor, control, or stop
in this life.
There are also things to
move toward, to desire.
This is the giving up game
with signatures and
everything.
To think without purpose
of food, violence, and
freedom.
I wake up and await
different messages. After
making sure no one wants to
have sex with me that
day, I eat, drink tea
and solve a few engineering
problems.
I'm moving my poems from
one aesthetic paradigm to
another.
It is hard to sing. Now I do
it 10% of the time. I go
to doctors to know if my
death will be painful.
Thanks y'all, this time I'll
not have a closure.
Lightly perfumed like

a slaughtered Russian
intellectual.
In the morning, traffic lights
seem to take longer.
Somewhere in this rhythm there
is a distance from things.
After everything is poorly
consumed, I wash my hands.
Day to day, all of us moving toward death,
the rational is
irrelevant.
Food, sex, etc., are mere violence.
God turns everything into
dust and back each
day.
It doesn't take much
to know our madness.

I receive two or three naked
pictures a month
from lovers at different
states of loneliness.
I am alone too and
now I have these
pictures.
Desire accentuates
loneliness.
We make plans to
meet that we don't
follow through on.
Each is happy
as is. With the
postponed promise
of intimacy.

A Final Note

Ramy's relationship to language is literal. When he reads he doesn't correlate a text to real life events or people. He can't read historically, he can't relate to an author's circumstances. All authors are created equal, and all are holy. The texts are just texts, all pouring from one place, all isolated from real-world events, they are not to be understood in relation to another domain, just in themselves. All texts are sin, all texts are absolute.

Afterwards: The afterword

Due to bad internal politics that was accumulating work stress, I collapsed in early 2019 with what is known as the cancer of mental illnesses, bipolar disorder. The bipolar disorder is composed of two phases, a manic phase, where I acted exactly according to the Mayo Clinic mania definition:

- Abnormally upbeat, jumpy or wired
- Increased activity, energy or agitation
- Exaggerated sense of well-being and self-confidence (euphoria)
- Decreased need for sleep
- Unusual talkativeness
- Racing thoughts
- Distractibility
- Poor decision-making—for example, going on buying sprees, taking sexual risks or making foolish investments

I thought of myself as Jesus Christ, and tried to mix the theory of the world being a simulation with a communistic way of creating it.

The suffering happens in the depression phase, where a severe sense of suicidal thoughts take place. Here are the symptoms of a depressive episode:

- Depressed mood, such as feeling sad, empty, hopeless or tearful (in children and teens, depressed mood can appear as irritability)
- Marked loss of interest or feeling no pleasure in all—or almost all—activities
- Significant weight loss when not dieting, weight gain, or decrease or increase in appetite (in children, failure to gain weight as expected can be a sign of depression)
- Either insomnia or sleeping too much
- Either restlessness or slowed behavior
- Fatigue or loss of energy
- Feelings of worthlessness or excessive or inappropriate guilt
- Decreased ability to think or concentrate, or indecisiveness
- Thinking about, planning or attempting suicide

I had to go to Egypt and get family support, which was good. I watched lots of tennis and I met the greatest erotic writers in the Arab world in a simple coffee shop in a semi-blue-collar neighborhood.

I eventually recovered and returned to the USA in 2020 where I experienced a relapse, another full bipolar cycle that destroyed even more friendships (in the manic phase) than the first cycle did.

While depressed, I started thinking about a writing project about Capitalism. Specifically about the software companies I know. I noticed that internal politics, which are usually conducted by higher-up managers who are not right for the job, cost the organizations millions or tens of millions of dollars. Capitalism sells itself to us as the best and most efficient system that can be. Numbers show otherwise. And if you start exposing these problems, there is no free speech—you will confront Stalinist-style restrictions.

I decided to write a memoir about child abuse, and how it constructed me, and how I confronted similar abuse in my experience in several software organizations, and how when Wittgenstein says that ethics and aesthetics are one and the same he is exactly on the money. My goal is to leave behind me a text that is accurate so that many people will see themselves in it. But more importantly I am hoping to propose ways to change the abuse in corporations and the loss it causes in money and resources.

Bipolar illness has offered me profound humility. I ask you to pray for me if you are the praying type, or to wish me luck.

Maged Zaher
Cairo, Egypt, 2022